Raccoon Island

The Encroachment of Man

Timothy F. McBride

Isolated on a lake island for untold centuries, an intelligent civilization of large raccoons must deal with mankind as they move westward in the New World.

Original Concept By
Shawn McBride

smcbride.zenfolio.com

authorHOUSE®

AuthorHouse™
1663 Liberty Drive
Bloomington, IN 47403
www.authorhouse.com
Phone: 1-800-839-8640

Published by AuthorHouse 11/26/2014

ISBN: 978-1-4969-3218-1 (sc)
ISBN: 978-1-4969-3576-2 (hc)
ISBN: 978-1-4969-3217-4 (e)

Library of Congress Control Number: 2014913885

EDITING

Coming up with a story concept can be easy at times. Putting it down on paper, filling in the blanks and meeting the printer's criteria is quite another task. Editing, as I had come to find out, is a big part of writing and can be very time consuming.

This story wouldn't be possible if it wasn't for the editing skills of Elizabeth Mottolese, Morgan McBride and the Cinelli Editing Company.

DEDICATION

This book is dedicated to:

My wife Melinda and my two children, Colin and Morgan,
who encouraged me to share this story with others.

The people of Lake Hopatcong
who keep the magic and
beauty of the lake alive.

My friends who gave me their honest
opinion during the writing process.

Contents

Chapter 1

The Incident at Nolan's Point

He was running for his life. The night was thick, cold and dark. The temperature had warmed just enough in the middle of February to bring a large thunder storm of cold driving rain that froze when it hit the ground. Everything not covered by snow had a crust of ice. What was once a beautiful layer of snow on the ground had now turned to a freezing mix of slush and mud. Fog, rising from the ice on the lake, filled the low lying areas.

There was a light in the distance. He hoped he could make it there. His pursuers were catching up fast. His heart was pounding. His breathing was heavy. His thick coat soaked up the winter rain weighing him down as he ran through the mud. His boots were big and clumsy. They were made to keep his feet warm not run through the night forest. Maybe the rain would hide his scent, he thought. It didn't matter. He left a trail of broken branches a blind man could track as he ran through the woods. The sound of thunder rolled across the lake. There was no moon shining on the frozen liquid landscape. The lake looked like a deep dark black hole just beyond the woods. On the edge of that abyss was that single light. He turned and looked behind him with a desperate expression on his face.

Lightning streaked across the sky lighting up the dormant winter forest. The eyes of his stalkers glowed in the flash of light. He was spotted. As he reached for his pistol he heard a thud. An arrow had pierced his right shoulder. The pain started to burn. With disbelief, he touched the bloody arrow head poking out through the front of his body with his left hand and he let out a yell that echoed across the lake. It had gone completely through.

There was no time to feel sorry for himself. He ran for the light. As he got closer he could see the lantern glow coming from a crooked wooden shack sitting next to railroad tracks. The small building was built out of scrap wood from shipping crates left on the side of the tracks. He knew it well. It was the trapping post by the Nolan's Point Train Station. All the trappers around Lake Hopatcong gather there to sell their furs and ship them back to the cities in the East. Nolan's Point is the last stop on the line. There are no roads around the lake. The railroad is the only way in or out of the area and the train doesn't run in February.

On this night, eight trappers from the lake area had gathered in the shack for a little company and to keep warm. Most of the men lived in tents or a makeshift lean-to on the side of a hill. The post was built by the trappers themselves and it showed. They were trappers not carpenters. As pitiful as the shack looked it was good to be in a dry warm structure. They had no idea what was unfolding outside in the dark.

A loud animal chatter echoed through the woods. He reached the door gasping for air. The front of his fur coat was covered with his blood that was dripping from the arrow head. He gave the door a shove with his left shoulder. It flung open and he fell to the floor of the shack panting and gasping for air. The light was dim inside but against the blackness of the night it had shined like a guiding star. The walls were lined with animal skins nailed to the wood. It smelled of tobacco and a hint of rotting flesh. A small black stove on the back wall was heating the structure. You could hear the occasional hissing sound of water dripping from a leak in the roof, landing on the hot stove and instantly boiling away. Inside, there was a beat up wooden table made of more shipping crate wood. On the table sat a home cooked loaf of bread and a brown bottle with whiskey in it. The bottle had no label. It was used for something else in its prior life. Now it holds someone's home brew. One of the trappers, sitting by the door with his chair leaning back on two legs was puffing on his pipe. He looked down at the man on the floor with annoyance. Rain and cold air were pouring in through the open door.

"Dutch, what are you doing?"

Dutch was just that, a Dutchman, who immigrated to America seeking adventure and riches. He made a living trapping animals and selling their pelts.

"Clos sa door!" Dutch screamed in a panic.

None of the men in the room could grasp the life threatening situation at hand. Nor could they understand Dutch's thick accent. Still wondering what he was doing and figuring he was drunk; one of the men stood up to close the door. Before he did, he stuck his head outside to check on the weather. He held his rough leathered face up to the night sky and squinted his eyes as the cold rain fell on his mug.

"Not looken good out here." The trapper said.

Then the lightning flashed and thunder rolled in the distance. In that moment of light the trapper saw the image of someone aiming a rifle into the doorway. He pulled back just in time before a bullet whizzed into the shack striking the pipe on the potbelly stove. The pipe fell to the floor in a clatter and the shack instantly filled with smoke and soot. The trapper slammed the door and locked it with a board across the frame. His eyes were wide. They were moving from man to man. He tried to make eye contact with someone, anyone. He wasn't sure if what he saw was real. They were all too busy coughing and covering their faces with their neckerchiefs. The only person not choking on the smoke and ash was Dutch. He was still laying on the floor in pain and complete exhaustion.

It was 1866. All the men, except for Dutch, were veterans of the war. They knew a gun shot when they heard it. Moving away from the window so as not to get shot, one man slid it open about three inches to let the smoke out. He then ripped an old beaver pelt off the wall and covered the window so anyone outside could not see into the shack. Two other men put their gloves on and reassembled the hot stove pipe so the smoke from the stove could once again vent outside through the chimney. Even with gloves on, the pipe was hot. They handled it like a hot potato trying to touch it as little as possible shouting "ouch!" and "ah!" as the heat passed through their gloves and to their skin. Some of the other trappers dragged Dutch to the center floor of the shack. Somehow it seemed safer in the middle of the rickety structure than against the thin wooden walls. Once the room cleared of smoke, their attention turned toward Dutch. No one had said anything yet but it was pretty clear. They were upset with Dutch for bringing what ever he was involved with onto them. Dutch looked up at the circle of weathered and angry faces that had gathered around him. Before the men could express themselves, a voice from outside shouted to the men.

"You in the shack, we have no quarrel with you. Give us the Dutchman and we will bother you no further."

The words were English but the accent was one they had never heard before. The men looked toward the door as if they could see through it. They were intrigued by the voice. Nelson, the de facto leader of the men, shouted back to whom ever was outside.

"How about we don't hand him over. What do you have to say about that?"

Nelson smirked and grunted. He looked at the other men for approval of his defiance with a big smile from his tobacco stained and rotting teeth. He always had a problem with people telling him what to do, even if he was going to do it anyway. Trapping alone in the woods was perfect for a man who had trouble with people telling him what to do. There was a slight pause. Then the voice from outside answered back.

"Well then trapper, you will meet the same fate as the Dutchman. It is of no consequence to us. We are not too fond of trappers. You have one hour to decide."

There was no emotion to the voice from outside. It was calm and confident. The men inside found this unsettling. Nelson pulled his pocket watch out. It was eleven minutes after nine.

"Now we know it's not the law that Dutch is in trouble with." One of the men stated.

Usually, the train station at Nolan's Point would have activity all night. However, it was the dead of winter. There was no one around except for the men in the shack and who ever it was outside hunting the Dutchman. The rain fell harder on the tin roof. Most people find the sound relaxing but not tonight. The men stood over Dutch as he laid on the dirty floor bleeding and wet. An argument erupted between them.

"You better come clean with us Dutch!"

Dutch knew why he was being hunted but he wasn't going to tell the men. If they actually believed the truth, they just might throw him out the door.

"I haf done nothink wrongk!" Dutch responded.

The circle of men around Dutch drew in tighter. Before the dispute could go any further, Red Feather came out from a dark corner in the shack. He was a Native American Nariticong. His ancestors had lived in the Lake Hopatcong area for hundreds of years before the Europeans started settling the area. Almost all the Nariticong had left the lake. Only a few remained. Red Feather was "civilized." That's what they called an Indian who was baptized as a Christian and wore the same clothes the white man did. He hunted and trapped the area as his ancestors had done. Taking only what he needed to provide for his family. He made friends with the other trappers who would help him sell his furs to the fur buyers. They called him Red Feather simply because he had a red feather in his hat. A feather that he had taken from the tail of a red tailed hawk when he was a boy. Nobody knew his real name.

The native parted the men with a wave of his hand as he walked over to Dutch. Red Feather knelt down next to the Dutchman. He slowly ran his hand across Dutch's fur coat. Despite the blood on it, the coat was a beautiful, thick, raccoon fur. There were no seams in the coat at all. It was one long continuous pelt large enough to make a long coat for a man. Red Feather had heard the recent rumors about Prospect Point. He knew the stories that were passed on from generation to generation in the Nariticong clans. It was a secret all natives from the area kept and never discussed with the white man. It was the reason why he refused to ever step foot on Raccoon Island. Red Feather stood up and looked at the other seven men.

"They have come for what is theirs. They have come for revenge. Dutch has brought death upon us."

Dutch knew exactly what Red Feather was talking about. The other men looked at the native with skepticism. Nelson looked at Red Feather with a smirk on his face.

"Now Red Feather, are you trying to tell us that ole Dutch here has brought some kind of injun curse upon us?" Three of the men chuckled.

"Why I bet ole Dutch here owes someone a gambling debt. Who did you stiff this time Dutch?"

The men chuckled again. One man, besides Red Feather and Dutch wasn't laughing.

"I saw who shot at us! It wasn't no man but it was wearing a fur coat just like Dutch's coat. There is something out there."

Boooom! It was perfect timing. The sound of thunder cracked across the sky adding weight to the man's claim. Red Feather grabbed Dutch by his coat and stood him up on his feet. The arrow twisted inside his shoulder. Dutch screamed with pain.

"Tell them where you got this fur! Tell them!" Red Feather demanded.

Dutch was too tired and injured to fight back. He just looked into Red Feather's piercing brown eyes and saw anger. He screamed in pain again.

"Da arrow iz stickink through me and Da Fur."

Red Feather pushed Dutch away from him. He pulled a large bowie knife from his hip and put the blade up to Dutch's face. No one was sure what was going to happen next.

"Turn around" Red Feather said with an emotionless voice.

The injured man just looked at him not knowing what was going to happen. Red Feather spun Dutch around and started to cut the arrow shaft sticking out of Dutch's back. Dutch was relieved the native's knife wasn't going into his chest but he still screamed with each saw of the blade. Red Feather then pulled the two bloody pieces from his body and passed them to the others so they could examine them. The flights on the arrow were made of turkey feathers. The shaft was made from a pine tree branch that was shaved straight. The tip of the arrow was a highly polished piece of iron shaped into a perfect doubled edged triangle. The density of the iron gave the arrow head a good weight. They could see that someone had hand forged it. There were hammer marks on it and it was very sharp. It was a well balanced arrow.

"Someone has made themselves a very nice arrow." One of the men said.

The men then took notice of Dutch's coat. Being fur trappers, they knew a good quality pelt when they saw one and Dutch's coat would catch a nice price back in New York City. A beautiful seamless pelt with gray, blue and black fur blending together. Obviously it was raccoon fur but where did he get such a large pelt?

After seeing the large pelt and the arrow, the men were willing to listen.

"So Red Feather, who has come to get ole Dutch here? We're listening."

Dutch piped in,

"Now holt on dare von secont! Are use going to listen to da fairy tales dis injun is going to tell you?"

One of the men pressed two of his fingers into Dutch's wound and pushed in. Dutch screamed in pain and fell back into a chair.

Chapter 2

A Mystery Revealed

Red Feather looked into the eyes of each man and he knew they were now ready to listen. He spoke with solemn seriousness.

"In this lake, surrounded by the deep blue water, there is an island covered with an ancient, dense forest. On this island, lives a tribe of man sized raccoons. They are far more intelligent than you may think. No one knows how they got there or when they got there, but they *are* there.

There's iron in these mountains. The Raccoons are hard and skilled workers. For centuries, the Raccoons have been taking iron ore from the mines on their island. By using fire and muscle, they craft it into anything from works of art to tools and weapons much like the white man has done.

Not many humans alive today have ever seen the Raccoons. Anyone with a boat can pass the island but won't see much through the dense forest.

"Hundreds of years ago, the area around the lake was home to the Nariticongs. They named the lake Hopatcong; which means "lake of clustered stars." The Nariticongs were strong and proud. Respecting life and all of nature was their way. The natives lived, fished and hunted along the shores of the lake. "They rowed their dugout canoes in the lake but always stayed close to the shoreline. Everything they needed was there.

The Raccoons had harnessed the power of the wind. They made sailboats to go on hunting trips. They would sail to the mainland to hunt deer and turkey to bring back to the island. The Raccoons were fully aware of the natives living on the main land. They were respectful of the natives. However, they had no desire to make contact with them. The Raccoons would use the darkness of the night to move about the natives without being seen. They would watch the Nariticongs in their daily lives. What they loved the most were the stories that humans told each other around the campfire or when they put their children to bed. Raccoons are always up for a good story."

The men in the shack listened intently as Red Feather told the story. What they didn't know was that their hunters had moved closer. The Raccoons were up against the shack unable to resist Red Feather's tale of their own past. Red Feather continued on and everyone listened.

Every so often the Nariticongs would see the Raccoon boats skimming across the lake. The boats were too far out and moving too fast for the natives to get a good look at them. They would never see anyone on the decks of the boats and no one was ever rowing them. Over time, the Nariticongs made up mythical stories that the boats were vessels of the *Manitou* or as you would say, the life spirits of the lake. This speculation and storytelling helped to explain the mysterious boats. It kept most of the tribe members at ease, except for one. A scout named Ahote. His name means, *restless one.* He was the adventurous type. This was quite the opposite of the rest of his tribe. Most men in his tribe spent time hunting and farming. They stayed close to the tribe. Everything they needed to survive was around them. Ahote has spent a lot of time away from his clan. He traded goods with other tribes. Everyone benefitted from his travels so the elders tolerated his ways.

Ahote stood about 5 feet 8 inches tall. His skin had a deep healthy tan color from years of being in the sun. He was lean and strong. All the walking and canoeing he did on his adventures left him in the shape of an athlete. Ahote was always restless. He wondered what was beyond the mountains and what was out in the lake. He had spent much of his time traveling among the many Lenape Indian tribes that lived between the Atlantic Ocean and the Delaware River. Although it was not the way of the Nariticongs to be so adventurous, his tribe loved their traveler Ahote. He would bring things back to the tribe from far away places. He would tell stories of all the things he had seen. He would use his skills as a traveler to trade goods with other tribes. He quenched his thirst for adventure and his tribe benefitted from it.

Ahote felt that he had traveled all he could by land and had seen all he could see between the Atlantic Ocean and the Delaware River. There was one adventure he had not been on.

He decided he was going to see what was beyond the shoreline of Lake Hopatcong.

One evening the traveler stood on the shore looking across the vast body of water. He was holding his hand across his eyebrows to shield his eyes from the sun that was setting on the distant west end of the lake. All he could see was water. It looked like the sun would set into the West end of the lake. Ahote's tan lean body stood out against the green forest backdrop. Little waves from the lake licked the shoreline he was standing on. He had seen many things in his travels. But as he stood there, looking across the glistening water, he couldn't help but wonder out loud, "what is out there?"

Now that his son Atoh was ten, Ahote thought it was time. He would take his son on his first adventure beyond the territory of the tribe. Atoh was excited. His imagination ran wild thinking of the things he would experience with his father. Little did he know that his imagination could never prepare him for the reality that was waiting for them out on the lake.

That night, Ahote spoke with Sakima, the chief. He entered the Chief's hut. The hut was made of tree saplings which were bent to form the frame work of a dome. The dome was then covered with tree bark. A hole was created in the center of the roof so smoke from the fire could escape the hut. There was a smoky haze inside that made it difficult to see across the room. It was dimly lit by a smoldering fire in the middle of the hut. In the dark shadows of the hut sat an old native with long silver hair that draped from his head down over his shoulders. He was wrapped in artfully painted deer skins. His face was weathered but he still had the eyes of a young man. They were sharp and they were reading the body language of Ahote. Sakima knew why Ahote was there before he spoke. The leader had an air of confidence and knowledge. He knew that Ahote would get an itch for another journey and would soon be standing before him. Ahote bowed his head in reverence as he stood before the great chief. "Speak brother", the chief said to Ahote.

"Sakima, I have traveled far. I have brought many good things to the tribe. I am asking your permission to take another journey."

"Where is it that you wish to go Ahote?" Sakima knew that his traveler had a restless heart. He did not think it was his place to keep him planted like a tree if he wished to roam.

"Sakima, I wish to venture out into Lake Hopatcong and uncover the lake's mysteries. I wish to catch up to one of the spirit boats and see it up close."

Sakima, not being an adventurous man himself and not wanting to leave the comfort of familiar territory, could not relate to Ahote's thirst for adventure. The wise chief did know that a successful trip by Ahote could only bring good things to his tribe and satisfy any thirst of adventure anyone else in the tribe might have.

After pondering the idea, Sakima spoke. "What if you make the boat spirits angry?" What if the spirits take their anger out on our tribe? Then what Ahote?"

The chief wanted Ahote to think about the people around him and not be selfish. He wanted to remind Ahote that he has responsibilities to his family and tribe. "Remember Ahote, our lives are not about us. They are about the people and things around us. Keep this in mind and you will come back to us. Go on your journey and return safely to us. Tell us your stories and find the secret behind the spirit boats. Do not anger the spirits."

Ahote was excited but he held his emotion in. "Thank you Sakima."

That night there was a big celebration. The Nariticong built great big fires. The women cooked a feast of venison and smoked fish. The men danced around the fires and asked the spirits to protect Ahote and his son on their journey. The children sang songs about Ahote the explorer. All the Nariticong did what they could to bring good luck to Ahote and his son Atoh for their journey across the lake.

As Atoh sat with his friends they speculated what things they would see. Ahote spent the evening with his wife. He was not sure when he would see her again. They were both used to this but it was still hard. Especially for Ahote's wife. They laid next to each other in the quiet darkness of their hut. The noise from the celebration outside was muffled by their hut walls. They spoke softly as they looked into each other's eyes. She loved her man of adventure but wished he would never leave her. The next morning, with Atoh at his side, the Indian scout packed his canoe with blankets, smoked deer and turkey meat, clothes and other tools he thought he might need and could trade while on their journey. Atoh's mother said goodbye to her son and husband. She was proud of them but she didn't want them to go. However, she knew she couldn't stop them. The two travelers said goodbye to their tribe. They rowed out into the lake. Their canoe sat low in the water because of all the supplies they had packed. It rocked back and forth until the two were settled in. Atoh felt as though the canoe would tip over but he didn't say anything. He trusted his father. It was going to be a long and slow journey. Many from the tribe stood on the water's edge and watched the two until they were tiny dots on the water. They rowed much further than any Nariticong had ever gone before. Eventually, they disappeared into the horizon. The only person left on the shoreline was Atoh's mother. A tear rolled down her cheek. Once again, she would be alone.

Chapter 3

Meeting the Raccoons

Much time had passed and the scouts had been rowing all day. The excitement of the trip had started to wear off for Atoh. He couldn't resist stating the obvious. "We have been paddling for a long time Father." Atoh's arms were growing tired. However, he didn't complain.

The young Nariticong kept paddling as his father instructed him to in order to keep the canoe straight. Ahote knew how Atoh felt. He too was tired. He smiled at his son. "Soon we will stop for the night."

The sun was a red ball, low in the sky over the lake. Even though it was late in the day, the heat from the low sun was affecting the two. The occasional splash from the paddle felt good on their hot skin. They were getting tired. Atoh was getting thirsty. His face muscles were strained from squinting. The harsh sun was reflecting off the water as it set. There was nowhere to hide from it. Ahote decided it was time to find a place to set up camp for the night. He wanted to get to shore and gather fire wood before it was dark. Atoh spotted a wooded island not too far off. "Finally," Atoh thought, "we can get out of this canoe." They decided they would camp on the island's shore and explore it in the morning.

They rowed their canoe up onto the rocky shore. Atoh jumped out and pulled the boat up further onto the rocks. The hollow wooden sound of the canoe echoed across the lake as it dragged across the stones. His father looked for a small area along the shoreline to set up their camp for the night. After stretching his legs and arms, Atoh went to gather wood for a fire. "It feels good to walk on land," he thought. "If my father and I are going to explore any more places after this, we need a bigger canoe." His mind started to wander a little bit as he dreamt of a giant canoe with men rowing it while he and his father stood on the front of it looking out into the open water. He liked the idea of other people rowing.

As he was looking for fallen branches and dead trees, Atoh thought it was odd he had trouble finding wood on the ground for a fire. "No one lives on this island," he thought. Where could all of the fallen trees and branches have gone? After finally gathering enough wood, Atoh never gave his observation a second thought.

Night had taken over day. The two Nariticongs sat by their fire and stared at the clusters of stars in the sky while the fish they caught earlier cooked on hot stones by the fire. Suddenly, Ahote looked into the dark woods surrounding them. In the edge of the tree line, he could see two eyes reflecting in the light. He motioned to his son without saying anything. Looking at the concerned expression on his father's face, Atoh knew there was a problem.

Both scouts slowly reached for their spears. "The eyes of men don't reflect light", Ahote thought. "What animal could this be?" Whatever was lurking in the woods was as big as a man. A black bear was looking to invade their camp, Atoh thought. He decided he was going to spear the mysterious creature. As he stood up and took aim at his target, a loud quick chattering noise shattered the silence. Several fur covered creatures, as tall as full grown men, appeared from the trees. All of them were wearing gleaming iron armor and all had fierce looking metal spears and swords. Seeing as he and his young son were out numbered and the beasts clearly had better weapons than he had, Ahote decided not to take the throw. He just stood there.

Atoh, with his eyes wide open in disbelief and fear, could do nothing but stare at the beings before him. As he was looking at them, the boy started to notice things. They were beasts, standing up straight and tall. They had large barrel chests and their arms funneled down to small black hands with claws. They were furry with dog like noses and they all had a band of black around their eyes. Was it paint or was it the color of their fur? Atoh whispered to his father. "Father, they look like giant raccoons."

The biggest of the beasts approached the two scouts. In Munsee, the native language of the Lenape tribes, he spoke to them.

"What are you doing on this island?" He demanded. Astonished that not only could the beast speak, but it could speak the language of his ancestors, Ahote just stared at the leader.

After Ahote composed himself, he answered the warrior standing before him. "We are Nariticong. We have traveled from the East shore to explore the lake."

Ahote went on to explain where his people live along the shores of Hopatcong. He told them how his people had never ventured far from the coast lines and he and his son were traveling to solve the mysteries of the lake. As Ahote went on with his story, the warriors, dressed in their fur and iron armor, began to relax. They haven't heard a good story in some time. Raccoons love a good story. Ahote spoke and the Raccoons fed the camp fire with wood. Both parties stood in the dancing light of the fire as the Nariticong told the story of his tribe.

When Ahote started telling the Raccoons of the mystical boats of the lake and asked them if they knew anything about them, all of the warrior beasts let out a chatter of hearty laughs, as a raccoon would do. It wasn't much like a human laugh at all, but the two Nariticongs knew they were being laughed at. The leader of the Raccoons put his arm around Ahote, as he was still laughing at him. "Come with us. We would like to show you something." The Raccoon warriors guided the two explorers through the dark to another area of the island.

The dense forest suddenly opened up. Before them was a lake side village of wooden huts and tree houses. Smoke slowly flowed from a few stone chimneys. Dim lights lit open doorways and windows. Raccoons, old and young, walked about tending to their various chores just as in any other village the two natives had ever seen. In the center of the village stood a great, tall, wooden building. It was built with giant round timbers that had the look of being cut and shaped with sharp metal. Torches hung off the corners of the building and a huge totem pole stood before the two thick wood doors to mark the entrance. It looked big enough to hold all the villagers at one time. At a dock, jetting out into the water, there it was! They saw one of the magical vessels floating in the water and tied up to the dock with ropes. It was a beautiful large wooden craft with shiny iron trim that glistened even in the moon light. It had a mast for the sails that was as tall as a tree. It could hold a lot more than the canoes the two were used to using. There it floated in the water before them. The vessel of the lake spirits.

The two scouts were astonished as they stood by the sailboat. Their hearts were pounding in their chests. It was far grander than the giant canoe Atoh had imagined. For generations, no one has ever been able to get this close to a lake spirit boat. They had never seen anything like it, at least up close anyway. When asked what kind of magic was used to move the craft, again the Raccoons laughed.

"Climb in and we will show you." One Raccoon said. By now, a crowd of furry villagers had gathered around the two humans. Some were sniffing them. A few reached out to touch them as if they were exotic animals in a petting zoo. Some looked at them with squinting eyes of suspicion. No matter what they were thinking, all the raccoons were polite to their guests.

The two scouts were guided aboard the boat. Torches along the gunwales of the boat were lit. A crew of Raccoons set the boat adrift and was preparing it to be under way. There was a flurry of action and Raccoon chatter. Suddenly a large sail was hoisted into the night air. It filled itself with the night wind and the boat moved away from the dock. In no time the crew had the magical vessel scooting across the lake. The torches were struggling to stay lit in the breeze. All you could hear was the water lapping against the boat and torches grunting with their flames. The two scouts had never experienced anything like it. They loved the feeling of speed and freedom the sailboat had given them. Atoh went to the bow of the boat. With the wind blowing on his face and his dark hair long hair fluttering, he leaned forward and extended his arms out as if they were wings. "This is what it feels like to fly!" he shouted to his father.

After a while, the boat returned to the island. The sails dropped quietly with a hish sound. The boat slowly turned and slipped into its spot with precision. Once docked, the Raccoon warrior invited the humans to stay on the island a few days and live with the Raccoons. Atoh asked if they could have more boat rides. The Raccoon reached out and gently touched Atoh's head. He could not deny the human child the simple happiness of a boat ride.

The Raccoons showed their guests the smelting process they used to make iron. There was a place on the island where a tall stone structure stood. Inside was a blazing fire. The heat could be felt across the field. It was the hottest fire the humans had ever experienced. They saw how the Raccoons fashioned raw iron into beautiful sculptures and strong tools. They also saw how the Raccoons ate raw meat and fish. This was odd to the Indians since the Raccoons had mastered such hot fires to smelt the iron. Apparently it never occurred to the Raccoons to cook their food.

Over the next few days Ahote and Atoh showed the furry creatures how to cook and smoke their fish and meat. This was astounding for the Raccoons. They loved the way venison and turkey tasted after being smoked. Being able to store meat this way would change the way they planned for the winter months. The humans gave the Raccoons some of the food they had brought along as a gift for being such generous hosts.

Weeks later, they returned to their village and told everyone of their great adventure. Ahote told his tribesmen of the Raccoons and their fierce looking warriors. He also told them of their friendliness and hospitality. The most important story he told was of the great wind ships the Raccoons sailed.

That one trip to Raccoon Island did not end the relationship Ahote had created with the Raccoons. A strong friendship between the two cultures grew. They traded goods and foods for hundreds of years. Raccoons would live among the Nariticong and Nariticongs would live with the Raccoons. They learned the ways of each other's cultures. The friendship was strong but secret.

Fearing that other neighboring tribes of Lenape Indians would not be as accepting as the Nariticongs, the chief decided that he and his tribe would never speak of the Raccoons to anyone but Nariticong tribe members.

If there was one thing the Nariticongs could do, it was to keep a secret. They were so good at keeping secrets that their whole way of living has almost been completely lost to time. All but a few can now speak Munsee, the language of the Lenape. No outsider, no historian and no archeologist ever heard of or found a trace of the Raccoons on the main land. There is no record of them ever existing, except for some iron tools that the Native American's had. Scientists and so called experts had misidentified them as Indian artifacts.

Chapter 4

The Nariticongs Move Out

In the year 1664, New Jersey officially became an English colony, at least as far as the English were concerned. Ahote and Atoh had grown old with their furry friends and passed on many years ago. They traveled the path all Nariticong eventually take, across the clustered stars of the Milky Way to the Sky World. There was a new generation of Nariticong and Raccoons living as neighbors on the lake. By sharing experiences in life, good and bad, a deep friendship had developed between the two civilizations.

However, there were now Europeans in the area. The Puritans settled in an area along the Passaic River called Newark. The settlers gradually migrated west and started having contact with the Nariticong. Hunters and fur trappers started venturing to Lake Hopatcong for wild game. Dutch settlers made some trading posts along the lake area to trade with the natives and trappers. They also started giving room and board to the people passing through on their way to the copper mines further west.

By the 1700's the Nariticong felt that the area was just becoming too crowded with European settlers. So they sold their land to the Governor of New Jersey and moved to Canada. When the Nariticong left, the secret of Raccoon Island left with them. For about one hundred years the Raccoons lived in secret on the island in the lake.

They would venture to the main land to hunt and to watch the European settlers in their ways. They listened to them speak and learned the language of the English, Dutch and Germans. After watching the settlers for a while, the Raccoons decided it was best if they didn't make themselves known. There seemed to be a certain amount of intolerance among the settlers for people who were different. What would they do if they met someone from Raccoon Island? So, as time went on, the Raccoons just went about their business and didn't mingle with the humans. From time to time there was a sighting of a raccoon. This led to myths of monsters roaming the forests.

Every now and then, a settler would manage to find his way on the island. This never worked out well. In fact, when these hunters and fur trappers saw a giant Raccoon, the first thing they would think about is how much money they would get for the giant fur pelts that the Raccoons were wearing. The trouble was, the Raccoons didn't want to give up their fur seeing as how it was attached to their skin.

These confrontations always ended with the settler getting killed. The Raccoons took the musket loaders and knives from the now deceased settlers and learned how to use them. After a while, the Raccoons made their own rifles and musket balls from their iron. They even managed to improve on the design that the settlers were using. They made musket balls pre loaded with gunpowder in a metal casing and a cylinder on the rifle that rotated the balls into the gun to be fired. This eliminated the need to load and ram every musket ball into the gun; which is what the humans were doing.

There was the problem of what to do with the settlers that invaded their island after they killed them. The Raccoons figured that since the settlers were going to eat them, they would eat the settlers. Raccoons didn't get much salt on the island. They loved the salty taste of the European settler's flesh. It was also fatty so it cooked well on their fires. The Raccoons knew enough not to make a bad habit out of eating settlers, so they only ate the ones that made it to Raccoon Island to cause trouble.

The years went on. More settlers came to the region. It became harder for the Raccoons to avoid the humans. The humans started mining iron ore from the near by mountains. They cut trees down and sent them to saw mills. In 1822, with the building of canals to connect Lake Hopatcong to cities, the lake became a busy place. The settlers started shipping iron ore on barges to cities like Paterson and Philadelphia where it was turned into farm equipment and steam engines among other things. The settlers even started cutting big pieces of ice from the lake in the winter. They would then float the ice through their canals and into the cities. In the cities they would store the ice in ice houses. Once the summer came, the ice houses would sell the ice.

The Raccoons saw the settlers doing this and found it funny. They thought ice was fun to play on, but to build a building just to store ice was something the Raccoons could not relate to. Lake Hopatcong was busy with commerce, but no one bothered Raccoon Island. Well, no one that lived to talk about it. The island remained clouded in mystery and myth.

Bam!

All of a sudden there was a loud bang on the tin roof of the shack. Red Feather had stopped telling the story to look up at the ceiling. Someone had thrown a large rock onto the roof. The men inside pulled their weapons as they looked up at the ceiling.

A voice yelled to them from outside. "Trapper, you have half an hour to give us the Dutchman. No one else has to get hurt."

Nelson, annoyed by the interruption, yelled out to their aggressors. "He aint comen out!" He then looked at Red Feather. "Now you go on and finish your story Red Feather."

The sound of thunder echoed loudly across the lake. The time span between the lightning and the thunder was much shorter than before. The storm was getting closer.

Chapter 5
The Legend of Samuel Colt

It was a cold night in late November of 1834. A full moon was shining over Lake Hopatcong. A man by the name of Samuel Colt was camping and fishing on the shoreline. Samuel was from Connecticut and from a family of industrialists. He was an adventurer, a tinkerer. He liked to experiment with firearms and ammunition. He was also working on a process to mass produce firearms and make the parts of his firearms interchangeable. He decided to take a break and go on a fishing trip to a lake he had heard about in New Jersey, Lake Hopatcong. While fishing along the shore, Samuel had spotted an odd looking sailboat skimming across the smooth water. It was a little too far off and a little too dark to see but he could tell there was great craftsmanship put into the sleek vessel.

Suddenly, a strong gust of wind caught the sail. The driver of the boat did not slack the sail to compensate. The boat turned over and capsized. Splash! In the moon light, Samuel could see a body fall into the water. He stood on the shore to look and listen for someone to start swimming or calling for help. He heard nothing. "Hello! Hello! Are you all right?" Samuel called out but there was no answer. Not wanting to see someone drown in the cold waters of the lake, Samuel ripped off his jacket, pants and shoes. Stripped down to his long underwear, he jumped into the water. Hitting the cold water made Samuel's body react unpleasantly. He had trouble controlling his breathing. His heart started pounding.

Samuel was gasping for air uncontrollably as his body tried to adjust to the shock of the sudden cold. The water being close to a temperature where it would freeze, felt like syrup as he moved through it. He kept gasping for air as he moved through the water. Samuel swam out to where he had seen the body fall in. There, just below the water's surface lay a figure motionless. He grabbed hold of the body and started to swim back to shore. Samuel's fingers and toes were completely numb. He could feel the numbness creeping up his body. "Whoever this is, he must have been knocked unconscious because he's not helping at all," Samuel thought to himself. It was as if he was dragging a giant sack of potatoes through the water. He just kept hold of what he thought was a fur coat, while trying to keep the person's head out of the water. As he swam to shore on his back, with his victim in tow, Samuel observed the large wooden sailboat slowly slip beneath the surface of the water and disappear.

Once they made it to land, he dragged the unconscious person up the rocky shoreline to his campfire. Shaking uncontrollably with cold, Samuel managed to put more wood on the fire to get more heat. He ripped his wet clothes off and wrapped himself in a blanket. He then went to his pack to get a blanket for the person he rescued. Soon, the fire was glowing with tall flames. In the flickering light, Samuel noticed that what he had pulled out of the water was not a human at all but some kind of creature clad in iron armor. "No wonder why he was so heavy." Samuel whispered to himself. Too tired and cold to really think about what he had discovered, Samuel sat by his fire to get warm. He was still shaking uncontrollably. His teeth were chattering. His arms and legs would not be still no matter how hard he tried. He stayed up most of the night feeding the fire so he and the furry creature wouldn't freeze to death. Steam slowly rose from beast as the heat from the fire evaporated the water from his wet fur. Samuel sat down and looked at him through the shimmering light of the fire. His chest rose and fell with each breath. He was still alive.

Since Mr. Colt was the tinkering and inventor type, he was more curious than fearful of the beast that lay before him. He took this opportunity to make an entry in his journal about his recent adventure of rescuing a giant woodland animal dressed in armor and sailing a boat that the creature himself probably made. He took careful study of the creature's features and described them in writing.

"It's a furry beast, the size of a man. It has a long snout, pointy small ears on its head and a black band of fur across the bridge of its nose and around its eyes. It has long thin fingers with black claws and paw pads. It appears to have an apposing thumb on its hand, just like a man does. Judging by the feel of its fur and the appearance of its face, it is a rather youthful creature." He wrote, "I have come to the conclusion that what I have with me is a giant raccoon that belongs to some sort of civilized societal structure and possesses intelligence. It also appears to stand upright and use tools." When Samuel read back what he had written, he himself had trouble believing it.

"No one will believe this," he thought. "Surely they will think I was drunk or crazy."

The frustrated man started to wonder if his experience was nothing more than a dream. He lay down by the fire, closed his eyes and went to sleep. Everything went black.

Samuel woke with a startle. He opened his eyes to find the furry warrior standing before him. "Wake up my friend!" The Raccoon spoke with an odd accent but in English. "I don't have much time but I wish to thank you for your courage and kindness. It appears by your supplies that you are alone. Are you alone?"

Not even daunted by the fact that the raccoon spoke English, Samuel quickly stood up. He thought about the answer to that question. "If I say I am alone will the creature attempt to eat me? If I say I am part of a party, will the creature run off not wanting to be discovered?"

"Yes, I am alone." Samuel could not help but tell the truth. "What do you mean you don't have time?"

"I can't linger too long on the main land during day light" the creature stated. "It will cause a stir."

"That's an understatement." Samuel said with a slight chuckle as he looked at the giant raccoon. He found it amazing that he was trying to reason with a raccoon. "Your boat has sunk my furry friend. You have no means of transportation."

"I will shed my armor and swim." The raccoon said with a bit of arrogance.

"Oh you surely won't be seen then." Samuel stated with sarcasm as he rolled his eyes. "Every boats man and trapper along this lake will be taking pot shots at you for your pelt!"

The raccoon examined his own body, remembering now that the very skin on his back was a prized possession to many humans.

"Stay in my tent and I will keep you sheltered until night fall." Samuel thought even if someone were to visit his camp unannounced, they would not enter his tent. "My name is Samuel Colt." "What is yours?"

"I am Leonidas." The raccoon exclaimed with pride. "My father named me after an ancient king warrior he heard about from a story told by settlers."

Samuel was shaking his head. "A raccoon named Leonidas. What is this world coming to?" He thought out loud. "Come in, and please, make yourself at home."

The tent was large and white with thick cotton walls. Fabric material made from plants was something the Raccoon had never seen before. It was soft and pliable like a deer skin but much lighter. There was also a folding cot and chair in the tent which were made of wood and cotton. Leonidas had seen similar human furniture before in his travels. He had no use for them. Raccoons preferred to sit in strong, big, wooden chairs and sleep on the ground. There was nothing like a good bed of leaves or pine needles.

Upon the condition that Mr. Colt remained in sight of the Raccoon, Leonidas agreed to take his hospitality. As the day went on, the two creatures of the earth carried on quite an interesting conversation. They found it easy to ask questions of each other and tell very personal stories of their lives when they were separated by the wall of a cotton tent. Samuel sat outside on occasion to smoke and tend the fire while his guest stayed out of view in the tent. For both of them, it felt good to tell someone about thoughts and events in their lives that no one else or very few knew about. They shared happy times and sad times.

Samuel learned about the Raccoon culture and the island. He learned that at night Raccoons come to the main land. They like to watch the settlers, as they call them. They like to sit in trees outside houses and campsites and listen to the stories they tell their children as they sit around their camp fires. That is how they learn the language of the humans. It was funny for Samuel to realize that the people of the area are being watched by these raccoons and they don't even know it. He learned how the Raccoons send hunting parties at night to the main land to hunt deer and turkey.

Before they knew it, the sun was low in the sky. The red ball nestled between two mountains on the distant west shore of the lake. "I need to get ready to leave" the Raccoon stated. My clan knows the route I would have taken. They'll come looking for me."

Soon it was dark. Off in the distance, the two could see a large sailing vessel with torches lit on its deck. It was moving smooth and silent through the water. When the ship got closer to Samuel's camp, Leonidas let out a loud raccoon chatter that echoed across the lake. Instantly, the ship changed course and started heading toward the shore where the human and raccoon were standing. By this time Samuel had a camp fire going that could be seen from the lake. It acted like a beacon for the boat that was heading their way. As the boat got closer, a loud chatter came from one of its unseen occupants. Leonidas picked up a burning log from the fire and waived it back and forth as he stood on the shoreline. Within minutes, the bow of the vessel was pulling up on the shore. It made a rumble sound as it shuffled through the gravel at the water's edge. Before the boat could stop, four warriors had jumped out and onto beach head. Their weapons were drawn. Their armor let off a low glow as it reflected the light from the fire. Their noses lifted up as they sniffed the air to see what scents they could pick up. One Raccoon stated with a sneer, "human." The others growled as they crouched down a little more and thrusted their weapons forward.

"This one is our friend," Leonidas stated. With that said, the Raccoon warriors put their firearms at their side. However, they still glared at Samuel with a deep stare of distrust. Leonidas told his comrades of how his ship had tipped and how Samuel risked his life to save him. Liking a good story as they do, the raccoons listened intently as Leonidas told them about what had happened and how he spent his day with the human. While the Raccoons were listening, Samuel was looking at their firearms. He could see they had fashioned long rifle barrels with wooden stocks much like the musket loaders of the day. He also noticed they did not have ramrods attached to their rifles and they had an odd cylinder by the hammer of the firing mechanism. Being a man who likes to tinker and a bit of a gunsmith, Samuel was fascinated by the rifles they had.

The Raccoons are creatures of gratitude. So, they decided to invite Samuel back to Raccoon Island for a feast of venison and turkey. They were happy Leonidas was safe. It was cause for celebration. Samuel quickly accepted the invitation. He put out his campfire, grabbed a small pack, his journal and hopped aboard the boat. The Raccoons pushed the boat out into the water and they quietly sailed off into the dark lake toward the island.

When they arrived at the dock, Samuel was greeted by curious onlookers. A crowd of the furry creatures had gathered. There was an odd mixture of the English language and Raccoon chatter coming from the crowd. Some were small and child like. Others stared at him as if he was an oddity from a foreign world. They stared, sniffed him and touched him out of curiosity. Even though they showed an overt interest to the newcomer, the Raccoons were still polite to their guest. They did everything a Raccoon could do to make a person feel welcomed.

Samuel was led to the Great Hall. Inside, it was a large spacious building framed with rough cut timbers. It had a high ceiling with thick wooden beams going across it. There were long wooden tables with large high back wooden chairs lined up along the sides of the building. Works of art made of hammered iron were hanging on the walls. One could tell they were hammered and bent by hand. They depicted scenes of Raccoons hunting with bows and wielding swords. In the center of the building was an open dirt floor. There was a large stone fireplace at either end of the building. Fires fueled by large timbers were burning in them.

As soon as they sat down, the food came out. Samuel spent the night feasting and talking with his new friends in the great hall. A fork and knife was set out on the table for their human guest. Raccoons prefer not to use utensils. Samuel and the Raccoons traded stories and ideas as the evening went on. Before the night was over, Samuel was introduced to one of the island's gunsmiths. Samuel knew a great deal about guns and had been experimenting with pre loaded musket balls. The two exchanged ideas and Samuel was shown how the Raccoons made their repeating guns. The craftsmanship of the guns amazed him. Each rifle was individually handmade. The gunsmith's pride in his own work was evident. He liked to put his own mark on the weapons along with other unique markings that made each one an individual. Samuel thought it was a slow process but it produced a fine firearm. "More like a deadly work of art" were the words he jotted down. Samuel took many notes that night in his journal.

Daylight was approaching. Although the Raccoons enjoyed the company of Samuel and his stories, they were a little weary of letting him go back to the main land. They feared he may tell others about them and their island. The raccoons made Samuel take an oath of secrecy. He was never to reveal to anyone what he had seen on this night. Samuel agreed. Leonidas then brought him back to his campsite before the sun came up. This made it difficult for Samuel to use landmarks to find their island. Once on the shore of the mainland, they parted as friends never to meet again. Years later Samuel would incorporate some of the mechanics he learned from the Raccoons into his own line of firearms that he would sell. The Raccoons never received credit for their inventiveness. Samuel took the secret of Raccoon Island to his grave.

Chapter 6

It's War!

It's now the year 1862. The Raccoons thought the humans had finally done it. Instead of fighting and killing each other a little at a time, they decided to have a war and kill a whole bunch of themselves at one time. The American Civil War had broken out one year earlier. Humans in the North were pitted in a battle against the humans in the southern regions of the land. The humans in the South had different values from their brothers in the North. They wanted to make their own country because of it.

The war was in full swing. Humans around Lake Hopatcong were busy mining iron ore to make war machines for the North. The lake was full of barges hauling iron to the cities of New Jersey where rifles, cannons and bullets were being made. The Raccoons did not like the traffic of the smoky steamships on the lake. The long slender steam powered boats, designed to navigate the narrow canal systems of the area, traveled day and night across the lake. This made it difficult for the Raccoons to travel by water. It made them uneasy. There was a lot of chatter on the island that it was only a matter of time before the humans would want to take the iron from the mines on Raccoon Island.

What the Raccoons didn't know was that some of the humans had that very same idea. Plans were being drawn up by the people of the North to start mining the island. What the humans didn't know is that the island is home to giant raccoons.

One summer day, while the morning sun was still low in the sky, a large flat barge, loaded with mining equipment and men from the Northern Army Corp of Engineers, landed on the island. They went up on the shore with such a racket that the whole island knew they were there. Within minutes of being on the island, the men of the North were cutting swaths of forest away from the water's edge. It was clearly their idea to just clear the whole island of every tree, as humans tended to do back then. As the men were cutting, plotting and setting up their equipment, they became aware that they were being watched. They didn't know by whom but they could feel the presence of someone else. A group of men was ordered to grab their rifles and venture deeper into the island to scout it out for any "hostiles." That was a word that the army used to describe anyone or anything that didn't agree with them or was in their way of getting things done.

As the band of men traversed through the island, they had a spooky feeling. Tall old pine trees sucked up the sun light before it hit the ground. The woods were thick and dark. Years and years of pine needles had piled up on the ground softening each foot step and creating an eerie silence. Large black crows were sitting in the trees and cawing at them like a bunch of watch dogs alerting their master to intruders. Something or someone was moving the brush around them. However, they couldn't see what it was. A rustle of undergrowth broke the uneasy silence. One of the men caught a glimpse of something quickly moving through the brush. Without hesitation, he pointed and fired his rifle in that direction. The other men, being scared, turned and fired their rifles in the same direction too. As they were reloading their rifles for another volley, it happened. Raccoons appeared from everywhere. They were in the trees and on the ground. The men looked on with fear as the fierce beasts approached them. They frantically started trying to reload their rifles. Pulling out a powder pouch and biting it open. Pushing the powder and musket ball into the barrel of their gun and then pulling out the ram rod to push everything down, getting the rifle into a firing position, pulling back the hammer, putting a firing cap on the hammer plate and then finally, aiming their weapon at their intended target.

On the practice range, a good soldier of the North could get three shots off in one minute. This wasn't the practice range. At the range they didn't practice shooting while having several angry furry beasts in armor plating staring them down. The soldiers didn't have a chance. They were so scared while they were reloading their rifles that most of them forgot to do one of the many steps required to make their weapon work. When it got to the point where it was clear that the intentions of the soldiers were to fire a musket ball into a Raccoon, the Raccoons opened fire with their repeating rifles. Within a matter of seconds and with scary efficiency, the Raccoons turned the small band of soldiers into an ineffective fighting unit.

Out of seven men, only one made it back to the shoreline and that was at the will of the Raccoons. He was badly wounded and stricken with fear. He could barely get his words out to the others. The engineers and workers had only heard the commotion in the forest hidden by the wall of ancient trees. They now stood over the injured man and tried to get information out of him but it was useless. He mumbled nonsense and pointed into the woods. "Sh sh sh sh. Ra ra ra ra." He had the look of fear that caused even the strongest man to become uneasy with the unknown that was just beyond the wood's edge. As they stood on the shoreline, they looked into the forest and then looked at each other. It was quickly decided that the best thing to do was to leave the island. That's what they did.

Now Alexander, the leader of the Raccoon guard unit that just had the run in with the Union soldiers, had a soft spot for humans. After all, a human had saved his brother, Leonidas, from drowning. He loved their stories and certain traditions of their culture. His parents had even named him after the great Macedonian conqueror, who, by the way, was human. Many of the Raccoons had names of characters from the stories the humans told each other and unknowingly told the Raccoons. It was from a human story that his father had heard many years before he was born. Alexander used to make his parents tell him the story over and over again.

He had to make a tough decision as they stood on the edge of the woods and watched the humans. "Do we let them go or do we kill them all?" It wasn't a decision Alexander took lightly. He stood there and pondered. He didn't have much time to make a decision. "If we let them go, the secret of the island could get out among the humans. If we kill them all we are no better than they are with their blood thirst." The decision was tough and one that would affect all Raccoons. The Raccoon leader then gave the command "stand down!" to his Raccoon guard. He would let the men go. Members of his unit looked at Alexander with bewilderment but it was not their place to question him. As he watched the barge of humans and their equipment steam off in a billow of black smoke, he feared his kind would regret his decision.

Later that evening, there was a meeting in the great lodge on the island. The elders and members of the Raccoon Guard gathered to decide what to do next. After much debate, it was decided. One elder slowly stood up and pounded on the large wooden table in front of him with his carved walking stick. The room instantly became silent. The elder scanned all the faces in the building and then began to speak. "It is unfortunate but inevitable that this day would come. Our way of life that we have maintained for generations would be threatened. We must take action as an act of self preservation. However we must act with responsibility. We will bury the human soldiers according to the customs we have observed the humans do. Alexander made the right decision in letting the remaining humans leave unharmed. It was civilized of him to do so. We must have hope that the Union Soldiers will leave our island alone. We will give the humans the opportunity to make the right decision on their own. However, we will prepare for the other."

The Raccoons were not foolish well wishers. They sent scouts out to observe the soldiers at their camp. The scouts would sit in trees and hide in the brush. They would listen to what the soldiers were saying and planning to do.

Back at the Union Army camp, the only surviving soldier from the incident on the island was questioned for several days. Major General George McClellan, who was in charge of the Union Army in the area, had trouble believing his soldier's statements of giant raccoons dropping from the trees with repeating rifles and metal armor. For hours, he and some of his commanding officers were in a small wooden cabin with the soldier and questioned him and his unbelievable story. It was as if the man was their suspect in the killing of his fellow soldiers.

It was, to say the least, an intimidating setting for the lone survivor with an outrageous story. There was one table and chair which the soldier sat at. A lantern hung in the middle of the windowless room. Three ranking officers stood over the man and demanded answers that they could believe.

However, no matter who or what was on that island, the army was now short six soldiers that had met their demise. If the Major General was anything, he was a man that cared for his troops. Securing the island to get the iron ore off of it was important to the war effort. Getting revenge for his six missing soldiers was a more pressing matter. A report was made by McClellan to be sent to President Lincoln in Washington D.C. by telegraph. The Major General of the lake operations surmised that they had encountered a group of unfriendly Indians living on the island. He requested permission from the President to use what force was necessary to secure the island so it could be mined for iron ore.

At the start of the war between the North and the South President Lincoln had all telegraph posts put under the control of the Federal Government. At a makeshift telegraph building put up on Lake Hopatcong. An army corporal versed in Morse code went to work right away sending the Major General's message.

Telegraph:

```
"Troops   report   furry   beasts   living   on
island.  Have  surmised  unfriendly  Indians
occupy  island.  Lost  six  men  from  survey  team
to  unknown  combatants  on  island.  Requesting
permission  to  use  necessary  force  to  take
island."
```

Within two minutes of the message being sent, the President held the deciphered note in his hand. He was busy managing the war against the Confederate Army. He often spent nights sleeping in the telegraph room he had installed at the White House so he could receive up to date information on troop activities and give almost instant orders to his generals in the field. The war was not very popular with a lot of people of the North and he was having a tough time against the South. After reading the report from New Jersey, The President sat down and thought about the incident. He knew he was fighting an unpopular war and didn't want to make things worse for his army by having it look like a bunch of conquerors kicking Indians off of their land. After all, he was fighting a war based on the principal that all men were created equal in the eyes of God and all men have an equal right to pursue freedom liberty and happiness. Was getting the iron ore this important? After days of thought, Lincoln decided to give the order for the army to take the island but to do it with great restraint so as to minimize casualties. Lincoln thought that a mere show of force may cause the Indians to talk with his general and a bargain could be reached where both parties were happy. It was to be a secret operation.

Telegraph:

"Major General, with great restraint, use what force is necessary to take the island. Diplomacy must be an option at all times. Remove all cameras and reporters from your camp. The greatest discretion must be used in this campaign. Lincoln"

Chapter 7
The Battle at Prospect Point

Once he got his orders, the Major General started to muster up all the soldiers in the area and draw up his attack plans. There is a piece of land that sticks out into the lake by Raccoon Island. It's called Prospect Point. The Schwarz family owns a farm on Prospect Point. The open fields of the farm run right up to the shores of the lake and the point sticks out into the lake by the island. It would make a perfect spot to gather the troops for storming the island. Well, at least McClellan thought so. The end of the point that connected to the mainland is covered with woods. The other three sides are surrounded by the waters of the lake. The point is also a hill that slopes toward the lake on the island side. Because the point is hidden by woods, the casual observer would not see the Union soldiers massing on the fields of the Schwarz farm. Hopefully the whole incident could be taken care of and no one in Northern New Jersey would even know what happened.

While the plans are being made and the troops are gathering, Raccoon scouts are listening and watching the

Union soldiers just as they have been watching and listening to the settlers of the region for hundreds of years, undetected. At night, the scouts would swim across the lake to Raccoon Island and report the activities of the human soldiers. They would then slip back through the water to their hiding spots on the point.

Once again, a meeting was called at the great lodge on Raccoon Island. Under the dancing light of torches, one of the elders stood and spoke, "It has become quite clear what the intentions of the humans are. If we let them land on our island with their army it will be disastrous for us. Even if we repel the attack, our secrets will be known. We will never know peace again. The humans will always be at our heels." After much debate and discussion, it was decided that a fight with the soldiers was inevitable. No matter what, they were coming. With this thought in mind, the Raccoons decided they will bring the fight to the Union soldiers.

Leonidas and Alexander were given the task of creating an attack plan on the soldier's camp. Killing humans was not something that either one of them looked forward to. However, it was their duty to follow orders and protect the Raccoon way.

The two Raccoon warriors looked at a map of the lake and the surrounding area. Their map was painted with various colors on the back of a deer skin that had been tanned over an open fire. It was turned into a scroll with two carved wooden handles attached to either end of the skin. Even though their map was not on paper or parchment, it still contained a great deal of detail about the area surrounding the lake. It was from this map that they created their attack plans.

The Union troops were gathering in large numbers on the point. Tents were popping up more and more in the open fields of the farm. It looked like a city of white denim and cotton tents. Camp fires dotted the landscape on the point. Supply wagons and cannons were being pulled onto the point by horses. Dirt paths were being worn into the areas of the fields where the soldiers kept walking. A mixture of dust and smoke hung over the encampment. It was periodically blown across the lake by a passing breeze. The scent of man would fall on Raccoon Island. All Raccoons, young and old could smell it and they knew that danger loomed.

The army that had massed looked impressive. However, that did not deter the Raccoons. They looked at the massing of the soldiers on the point as their opportunity to strike a crippling blow to the Union Army. There was only one way for the soldiers to retreat off the point. That was through the wooded area that connected the point to the mainland. Since the other three sides of Prospect Point are surrounded by water, the Raccoons could use their sail ships off the shores to get in close and undetected. Their archers would then be close enough to launch arrows into the camp.

Even though the Raccoons had mastered the art of making firearms, many of them still preferred the silence of edged weapons and the bow and arrow. Archery was a skill they had maintained in their culture for over a thousand years. They also knew that a silent hail of arrows would be what they needed to maintain the element of surprise.

Two units were created. One unit of Raccoon Guards would sneak ashore and wait in the woods where the point and the mainland connected. Their job was to cut off any retreat from the point and to stop any effort from other Union soldiers to reinforce the troops there. The second unit of Raccoons was to be on several ships that surrounded the point. Once close enough, they would launch a barrage of arrows into the camp to start the attack and weaken their enemy before any Raccoons came into contact with the humans. If they were to defeat this army of men, surprise and stealth needed to be part of their plan.

The time to attack was upon them. It was the time of the month when there was no moon in the night sky. Their ships would not be seen. To ensure this, the Raccoons took all the metal parts off of their ships that they didn't need. This avoided any light reflecting on them or unnecessary noise. They also dyed their sails black so they would blend in with the night sky.

Once it was dark and the human's had started to settle down for the evening, the dark vessels set sail from the island to surround the point. The other unit of raccoons quietly paddled across the lake on planks of wood as wide as tables. Along with them, they carried their repeating rifles, ammunition and short swords; taking caution to not get them wet. Once in the shallows of the mainland, they quickly moved from the water into the tree line.

The Raccoon guard came across a few soldiers who were monitoring the road into the Union camp. The soldiers were quickly and quietly dispatched by the cold steel of the Raccoon's swords. They now had control at the base of the point between the camp and the mainland. The guard took positions among the trees and waited.

At the Union Army camp, no one knew what was about to happen. The soldiers were so confident that they would rout the Indians from the island and that they were a superior fighting force. The only guards posted were at the base of Prospect Point. They had not posted any guards around their camp nor did they have any concerns of attacks from the water. Soldiers sat at their fires and looked up at the clusters of stars in the moonless night. Many others lay in their tents and slept or read a book by the light of a lantern. There was the sound of music as someone played a fiddle and sang songs.

Then it happened. A loud chattering sound echoed across the lake and through the point. It broke the calmness of the evening and caused all the soldiers to pause for a moment. The raccoons on the mainland were now in position and that was the signal for the attack to begin. The dark wooden ships slowly and quietly moved into arrow range of the camp. The Raccoons on the ships pulled back their bows and launched their first salvo of black arrows into the night sky.

So many arrows had gone into the air; the soldiers could no longer see the stars that were hanging in the sky. Before the men of the North could realize what had happened, a storm of arrows had fallen onto the camp. That first round of arrows left carnage of dead and injured unsuspecting soldiers. It got the surviving soldiers moving. Many ran for cover in their tents and many grabbed their rifles. When the second round of black arrows fell on the camp, the soldiers soon realized the hard way that a tent was not a good place to get cover from an arrow attack.

It was chaos. Sergeants and lieutenants were trying to organize their men into fighting squads. Men were tripping over their fallen comrades. The artillery men were trying to roll their cannons by hand to set them up. They were not too sure where the enemy was but they knew they were upon them. Even though the Union army was engaged in war with the South, many of the men on Prospect Point had never seen action before.

The Raccoons, being nocturnal by nature, have excellent vision at night. From the ships, they could see the men moving about on the open fields. They were easy targets. Standing by a cannon was a death sentence for the soldiers. Any time a group of men tried to set up a cannon they were met with a hail of black arrows. One sergeant did manage to get a group of ten men onto the edge of the field where they could see the ships sitting out in the water. He looked at his men behind him and yelled,"Follow me lads if ya want to live!" He was a battle hardened Irishman that had spent many years in one army or another. His years in the Crimean War as a soldier of Britain had taught him a few things. "What are ya standin there for lads? Give me two lines!" Forming two rows of five and using their rifles, they fired a volley of .58 caliber balls into one of the dark vessels. The ship was so close to the shoreline that the soldiers could hear their mini balls strike the wood and metal of the ship. They could also hear the grunts of the Raccoons as several of the archers were struck. A cloud of gunpowder smoke hung around the ten men. "Alright lads, run! Fifty yards to the right and form up again!" The sergeant barked orders out from under his handlebar mustache and kept his men focused. He quickly moved them to a new location before the archers could bear down on them. Once they reloaded, the sergeant gave the order to fire. The small band of men fired again into the vessel. Flattening out on impact, the .58 caliber mini balls made of soft lead ripped through the flesh and crushed the bones of the Raccoons standing on the ship's deck. They tore into the light pinewood body of the ship. Those raccoons lucky enough to get hit in their body armor only suffered minor injuries. Others who were hit in the arm, leg or head suffered fatal wounds.

Once the men knew where the vessel was, it was an easy target to hit. The captain on the ship let out a loud chatter and the ship made a hard right turn to put its back to the men on the point. As the ship tilted into her turn, blood flowed across the deck where he was standing. The captain knew he needed to reposition his ship and leave the fight for now.

Black arrows still rained onto the open fields of Old Man Schwarz's farm. There was no where to hide. A modern army of the 1800's was just not equipped to repel a major arrow attack. Major General McClellan could see the tragedy unfolding. Not wanting to lose any more men, he ordered a retreat. The bugle sounded and the men started to head for the woods. As they ran into the tree line for refuge, the second stage of the Raccoon's plan took place.

On the ground and in the trees laid Leonidas and his raccoon guard with their repeating rifles. When the soldiers hit the tree line, they were met with a volley of fire from the raccoons. Instantly, dozens of men dropped to the ground in the wooded area. In a panic, the men ran back to the field at the tree line. A cloud of gun smoke slowly moved from the woods and passed over them like a ghost. This army of men was not trained for such a battle. They were taught to square off against their enemy in an open field. Once in the clearing, one of few lieutenants left alive formed a line with his men. They loaded their weapons in an orderly fashion at the command of the officer. He then yelled, "fire!" A volley of mini balls rocketed into the trees. The men could hear their bullets hitting something. They had no idea what they were shooting at or where their target was. However, usually when a squad of men shot their rifles into the same general direction, they tended to hit something. That was not the case this time. Knowing the men would return fire in this fashion, Leonidas ordered his warriors to climb into the trees. No Raccoon was on ground level.

By this time, some of the ships had come ashore. The other unit of Raccoons was working its way across the fields of the farm and the encampments of the Union soldiers. It was an arduous battle for the Raccoons once in the open field. There were losses on both sides but the Union Army had already lost more than it could absorb through the sneak attack. The Raccoons had captured many men. The prisoners were forced to walk across wooden planks and board waiting boats. They finally got to the edge of the point where the last remaining union troops were battling the Raccoon unit in the woods. Fighters had fallen on both sides of the skirmish. However, the humans were taking far more losses. Open field fighting tactics that were so popular with European armies of the day were just not working in the woods of Prospect Point. With the second unit of Raccoons at their back, the men were unable to retreat. Even if they did, it would be into the dark waters of the lake.

Alexander grabbed one of his new prisoners by the front of his shirt and lifted him up off the ground. "Tell your major general, if he and his men would like to live, it would be in his best interest to surrender," he snarled at the Union soldier. Alexander threw the man toward the direction of the last remaining human soldiers fighting. After just being threatened by a giant talking raccoon, the soldier didn't know what to think. He laid on the ground in disbelief. He then got up and ran toward the remaining soldiers.

By this time, Major General McClellan had received several reports stating that their attackers were some sort of furry beasts. Nothing could be confirmed. They had not taken a body or prisoner of their adversary during the battle. As the man, who had just left Alexander's position, approached the Major General, McClellan could see the fear in his face. "Major General! Major General!" the man yelled. "We have been over run by giant raccoons! There's a large unit of them just over the crest! They are armed with rifles, swords and armor! The leader stated that they intend to take us if we don't surrender!"

Just as the man was finished talking, something caught the Major General's eye. A unit of beasts was moving rapidly across the field and taking up positions. They were looking to cover both flanks of the remaining Union soldiers. They were in a bad position. The Major General was a caring man. Some would say he wasn't cut out for leading men into battle. He cared more for the well being of his troops than he did of winning a battle. As noble as this may be, it could get in the way of fighting a war.

McClellan thought to himself. "What monsters have we awakened? The beasts never bothered anyone until we went on their island. If we surrender, there is a chance we can get out of this situation alive. Maybe all they want is to be left alone." McClellan yelled, "Cease fire! Cease fire!" The order was passed down the line of men. "Cease fire! Cease fire!" sergeants and lieutenants yelled. Smoke hung over the men who were lying on the field. The Major General looked at one of his aids. His eyes were big and watery. With a shaky hand, he pointed to the man as he looked down at the grassy field. The order was given, "raise the white flag."

The men were silent. As the gunpowder smoke was clearing, the Union soldiers could see the outline of their enemy moving into the clearing under the night sky. They were stunned by what they had seen. "Army of the North, drop your weapons and your lives will be spared." This order came from the ranks of the raccoons. The men, still in disbelief, laid down their weapons as they stared at their enemy. There before them stood an army of beasts clad in armor, holding rifles and carrying short swords in scabbards on their waists.

It didn't take long for the raccoons to round up the remaining soldiers and board them on sailboats waiting in the lake. A table and chair was brought up to the field where Leonidas, Alexander and McClellan were now standing. The Raccoon leaders sat McClellan down in the chair at the table. They gave him water and then spoke of the terms of surrender. Leonidas slammed his fist onto the table and put his face uncomfortably close to McClellan's. As he showed his teeth he said, "All we wish is to be left alone on our island. Nothing more, nothing less." Tell your President Lincoln that we seek no trouble with the humans. He can have any other piece of land around this lake but not Raccoon Island. It is not yours." McClellan stared at Leonidas. He couldn't believe that such creatures existed and that they had an army skilled enough to attack him and his men in such a manner. McClellan uttered, "We thought there were Indians on the island." Leonidas pulled his head back and squinted with disgust at the Major General.

"Are Indians, as you call them, less deserving than you or I of the land their ancestors tended to?"

Leonidas looked down his nose with disdain at the man sitting before him. It was at this point he realized that he too harbored a prejudice just like the human. He realized he viewed

Raccoons and Native Americans as superior beings to these settlers. It was unsettling for him.

Fearing the worst, the Major General asked in a shaky voice, "What will you do with my men?"

Alexander chimed in, "Until we feel sure your president will leave this island alone we will keep your men as ballast on our ships." Alexander then motioned to a ranking Raccoon warrior standing by him. The officer left to insure their prisoners were rounded up and ready for transfer to the waiting boats. At the other end of the point, a line of men prepared to walk the plank onto the ships. They were searched and stripped of all weapons, knives, belts, shoes and any other items the raccoons deemed not a necessity. Barrels of contraband were shipped to Raccoon Island so that they could be studied by the Raccoons. The Major General was also kept as a prisoner. A mass grave was dug on the farm land. The bodies of the fallen human soldiers and their weapons were placed in it and then buried. The site was marked on a map by the Raccoons.

A line of men were marching into one of the vessels. As one of the men walked by a Raccoon standing guard, they locked eyes. Feeling challenged by the man, the Raccoon walked over to him and struck him in the ribs with his rifle. The Raccoon snarled at the man as he lay on the ground, "what are you looking at human?" The Raccoon never saw it coming. With a left uppercut, the old Irish sergeant struck the Raccoon on the underneath of his snout. Like dogs and other animals with long noses and a keen sense of smell, the nose of a Raccoon is a sensitive place packed with nerve endings and olfactory sensors. The Raccoon left his feet and fell to the ground on his back. His sight was blurry. Pain shot through his head. For a moment, the raccoon could not tell up from down.

The Irishman stood over him with his fists up before him in a fighting stance. "If it's trouble you want, it's trouble I'll be given ya. Stand up and let's settle it like men." The sergeant paused. He forgot who was before him. "Well ya know what I mean." Before another word could be said the sergeant was surrounded by Raccoon guards. Their swords dipped slightly into the flesh of his arms and chest. He put his fists down as he scanned the eyes glaring at him. He got the message. "Well fellas, I guess every regiment has one. We have our fare share of troublemakers too. I'll be steppen back in line now." The Raccoons couldn't agree with the sergeant more but they weren't going to tell him that. The Irishmen walked over to the man lying on the ground. "What are ya lying there for lad? Get up. Make your mother proud now." The sarge helped the man up. "Belly in, chin up, shoulders square. There'll be no slacken." The sergeant continued to bark at the men until the sound faded as they walked into the belly of a waiting ship. He knew if the minds of the men were occupied with his voice and he was dishing out some discipline it was less likely another incident would occur.

By the time the sun rose for the new day, all the soldiers were gone. Nothing was left on the battlefield but a few smoldering campfires and some trash scattered about. The details of the

Raccoons demands were written down on paper and sent to Washington D.C. with one of the Major General's officers on horse back. It would take three days for the man on horse to make it to the capital. In the mean time, the dark ships, filled with prisoners, set sail for an obscure cove in the lake.

Chapter 8

Lincoln Meets the Raccoons

It was a beautiful sunny day in Washington. The morning sun shined through the windows of President Lincoln's office. It warmed his room nicely. However, Mr. Lincoln could not enjoy the day. Just beyond the boundaries of the capital city lay a battle line. The North and South were entrenched along a line of war that separated the United States of America and the Confederate States of America. Each day the war continued was another day of frustration and pain for the President. It hurt him to see his nation being ripped apart. As he stared out the window, a great sense of sadness and anger filled him.

Suddenly there was a commotion outside the President's office. Men were yelling. Then, Lincoln could hear the sounds of boots running across the floor. The door to the President's office swung open. Standing in the door way was a lieutenant from the Union Army. He was covered with dust and breathing heavy. His uniform was ripped. Right behind him were the guards of the President. "Mr. President, I have news from New Jersey." One of the guards walked forward and handed the

President a leather pouch. Lincoln looked at the men for a moment. He scanned each one of their faces. Their eyes were wide open. They were looking at him like children waiting for comfort from their father. The President took the beat up leather pouch and walked over to his desk. Inside was the parchment that contained the written demands of the Raccoons. Lincoln placed it on his desk and looked toward the dusty soldier.

The President spoke. "Tell me Lieutenant, what news do you have for me from New Jersey." Lincoln knew of the operation that was to be conducted on an island in Lake Hopatcong. But how could that cause such urgency? The president thought.

The soldier was given a glass of water by one of the butlers. He gulped it down. The water that splashed on his face and boots cleaned the dust from them. He then began to tell the President the story of the battle that had taken place just days earlier. After hearing the report his soldier had given him, the President sat at his desk and opened the pouch and read a letter from his general.

Mr. President,

We have engaged a formidable enemy in battle at Prospect Point along the shoreline of Lake Hopatcong. Our men fought bravely but they were not victorious. After seeing that the battle clearly could not be won and that further fighting was futile I gave the order to surrender in the hopes of preventing further loss of life.

Our adversary, it turns out, is not a group of native Indians but rather a civilization of intelligent large furry beasts that appear to be very raccoon like. They have made it clear to me that they have no intentions of expanding their territory beyond the boundaries of the island they currently live on. The beasts are holding many of our men prisoner on ships in the lake. The conditions of their release are as follows.

1) The United States recognizes Raccoon Island on Lake Hopatcong as a sovereign state.
2) The United States agrees never to attempt to mine the iron ore on Raccoon Island.
3) The United States or any of its lesser governing bodies will never attempt to encroach on Raccoon Island.

If these three mandates can be agreed to then our men will be returned to us.

Respectfully,

Major General George B. McClellan
United States Army

While the president read what was written down, the room was silent. By this time, some of the President's military advisors had gathered in the room. As he sat at his desk and read the signed surrender of Major General McClellan and then the demands of the Raccoons, a rage filled the man who is usually calm. Lincoln stood up and screamed as he cleared everything from his desk with one swipe of his long arm.

He looked at the dusty man standing before him. "Man sized raccoons you say Lieutenant."

"Yes, Mr. President. I wouldn't believe it myself if I didn't see it with my own eyes, sir." The soldier stated.

This is the second time the President had heard of giant raccoons on this lake in New Jersey. He had read the report of the incident on the island and the statement given by a soldier stating that he and his comrades had met up with weapon wielding raccoons.

The war with the South was not going well for the President. He was getting pressure from politicians and the public to bring it to an end. Many officers of his army were already treating the South as if it were foreign soil. The last thing he needed was another war.

"Let's get ready for a trip to New Jersey." The President shouted. "Send word to Major General Grant. He is to meet me there."

Raccoons or not, the President was disappointed to see Major General McClellan's signature on a surrender. Lincoln had met with Grant several times before. The President was impressed with Grant's tenacity and self reliance. Ulysses Grant didn't know it at the time, but this meeting with President Lincoln would eventually cause him to be commander of all Northern Armies during the Civil War.

As luck would have it, Grant had just sent a message by telegraph wire reporting his status and troop movements. He currently was in charge of the Union Army of Tennessee. He had been defeating the Confederates along the Mississippi River. Mr. Lincoln's advisors were able to send a message back.

Telegraph:
"TO MAJOR GENERAL GRANT, BY ORDER OF THE PRESIDENT, YOU ARE HEREBY COMMANDED TO RENDEZVOUS WITH PRESIDENT LINCOLN AT PENN STATION IN NEWARK, NEW JERSEY."

It took two days for General Grant to travel by train from Tennessee. Once he arrived at the Newark train station, he met with President Lincoln, who was in the presidential railroad car.

The car sat in the train yard among other cars. It stood out as something special. The railroad car the President road in was not only full of safety features to protect the President; it was a work of art. The outside of the car had hand carved wood accents that meshed perfectly with the steel frame of the car. Plates of steel hung low on the car to cover the wheels. There were only a few windows on the car. They were covered by thick wooden shutters that opened from the inside. Built into the car were three holding tanks. One held fresh drinking water; another held kerosene to burn for light and to heat the car in the colder months. The last tank was for the bathroom. It held the waste water. The walls of the car were four inches thick and so were the doors to access it. Inside, there were two elegantly decorated rooms. A bedroom with a large bed and closets. Paintings hung on the plush upholstered walls. There was a grand living room with beautiful furniture and a large desk for the President to sit at and work. Most of the furniture was secured to the floor of the car. The kerosene lanterns and heaters were built right in the walls. There was also a pantry with provisions for several days.

Grant stood in the entranceway of the splendid train car. The man and machine were in great contrast. He was a rough looking man with an unkempt look. His uniform was dusty and slightly wrinkled. His beard needed to be trimmed. He had a rugged, weathered look on his face as if he spent most of his life out in the elements. The Major General took in the beauty and craft-man ship of the rail car. He had spent the last few months of his life living in sparse quarters overseeing the distribution of cotton purchase licenses to merchants from behind a beat up wooden table in a dusty out building that was full of bullet holes. After the fighting, there was not much left in the way of elegance in the cities he now controlled along the Tennessee and Mississippi Rivers. He would have liked to have had the President's rail car where he was.

"Come in Ulysses." The President stated as he extended his hand for a handshake. The two men shook hands and gave each other a warm look. Both had come from a modest upbringing and often felt uncomfortable around the elites of society. They were comfortable around each other however. Lincoln poured some water into a wash pan and set a towel aside. He then motioned for Grant to freshen up.

As Grant took advantage of the hospitality, the President started to tell the Major General of his most recent dilemma.

"Ulysses, we have a problem up here in New Jersey. While attempting to expand the iron ore mining project northwest of here, our troops have stumbled upon an obscure indigenous colony on a lake island. Getting them off the island so it can be mined has proven to be tougher than they thought."

The Major General was listening. At this point, he only had a small part of the story. The President went on with his briefing of the reports of beasts carrying weapons and being organized. When he told Grant about the battle that had taken place at Prospect Point and the result of the battle, Grant stood up from his chair in disbelief. The Lieutenant who was at the battle and who delivered the message to the President was escorted into the presidential car. He proceeded to give Grant details of the battle as they looked over a map of the region in question. Grant also looked over a peace treaty proposal that the Raccoons had drawn up.

When all was said and the Major General had all the information, he looked at Lincoln with a squint in his eyes.

"Where do you want to go from here Mr. President?"

The President responded, "What are my options Mr. Grant?"

Grant walked over to the map wall. He flipped some maps over and ran his finger across the Morris Canal and various rail lines.

"Sir, by using the Morris Canal system we can send some navy war ships used on the Mississippi River around Florida, up the coast and then up the Delaware River. They can get through the canal system and into Lake Hopatcong. We can lay siege to the island and soften it up with cannon fire. After that, we can send in a larger force to take the island. This can all be done in a little more than a month."

There was a pause as the men in the room thought about the attack plan. Grant however, was thinking about the Mexican War. He was successful in that campaign and had pushed his troops all the way to Mexico City. It left a bad taste in his mouth. It was his opinion that the U.S. took advantage of a weaker country simply because they could. Oppressive government went against what the founding fathers of United States had fought for. Fighting the Civil War to preserve the Union was a worthy cause. Fighting a small group to take their land for iron ore was not a worthy cause in the eyes of Grant.

Grant spoke up again. "Mr. President, there is another option. We could sign a peace treaty with these furry creatures, these raccoons." The President sat back in his chair with a smirk on his face.

"It's funny hearing that come from the mouth of a career soldier, Major General."

Grant smiled back. "Sir, the last person who wants to go to war is the career soldier."

The fact was that the President was already fighting an unpopular war. He did not need a second front with a new enemy in the woods of New Jersey. If he could settle this issue diplomatically and move on, that would be just fine for him and his re-election efforts to be president again. The people of the North were tired of war. The President stood up.

"Then let's work out the details and get this treaty on paper. I have men sitting on boats as prisoners somewhere in Lake Hopatcong."

It was risky. No one really knew what to expect of the Raccoons. Major General Grant had never seen them and wasn't sure if he was ready to believe such a thing could exist. They had to take a chance. More war was not the answer. Plus, all the Raccoons required of the U.S. was to just let them live in peace.

That night, in the President's rail car, Grant and Lincoln put the details of the treaty onto paper. Two copies were handwritten by Grant. It was decided that the treaty would be a secret. People were not ready to accept the fact that giant raccoons walked the earth. The soldiers who already knew about the Raccoons would have to be sworn to secrecy. From there, the only people that would ever be told of the treaty and the existence of the Raccoons would be the President of The United States. The men decided the secret would be passed on only from president to president. In time, only the President would know. What they didn't know was that this would be the first of many presidential secrets that followed as the nation grew older.

By sun up the next day, Major General Grant had secured a stage coach, a team of fresh horses and five well armed men. With the assistance of the lieutenant who was at the battle, they were getting ready to head out to meet the Raccoons. President Lincoln exited his train car. He was dressed in common clothes and a deer skin coat. Grant looked at him. He knew right away what the President was thinking.

"I don't think it's wise that you come with us Mr. President."

"Nonsense Ulysses. Besides, I want to get a look at these creatures for myself."

The president never thought too much about his own security. He always moved about without guards. This would, someday, be his undoing. The Major General wasn't going to argue with the President of The United States. Plus, he had enough men with him to keep Mr. Lincoln safe. Off they rode.

The westward roads toward Lake Hopatcong were in good shape and easy to travel on. The men made their way to Dover, New Jersey where they boarded a wooden barge with their horses and gear. From Dover they continued west through the woods of western Morris County on the Morris Canal.

The Major General sized up the canal as they floated through the forest on the man made river wondering how his river gun boats would fare the trip to the lake. By sun down they were steaming across Lake Hopatcong on a slender paddle boat. The seven men stood on the boat and took in the natural beauty of the lake. As the sun was setting on the western end of the lake it lit up the clouds in the sky to beautiful shades of pink. President Lincoln looked across the open view and felt compelled to comment.

"It's just beautiful up here. Would you agree Major General?"

The General had seen many parts of the country. He looked at Lincoln and said, "I do agree Mr. President. This lake is a hidden gem."

By nightfall the band of men landed on the shore of Prospect Point at the Schwarz farm. Once there, General Grant and two men rode their horses to the farm house and knocked on the door. They spoke with Old Man Schwarz. Mr. Schwarz was a friendly man eager to help weary travelers. He let the group of men set up lodging in one of his out buildings on the farm. The one room building reminded Grant of his post in Tennessee, minus the bullet holes. They were able to gather some boxes and crates from around the farm to make makeshift chairs and writing areas. A single lantern hung from a beam in the ceiling. Through the cracks in the planks, the men could see the light from the farm house. Later that evening the farmer came out to check on his guests. They were well supplied and had cooked themselves a nice dinner.

Mr. Schwarz stared at Lincoln and said, "I think we have met before. You look familiar sir."

Lincoln gave the old man a gentle smile and said, "I get that a lot."

The men asked the farmer about the soldiers that were on his land. Old man Schwarz just shook his head. "I don't know what those fellas were up to. One night, they made a lot of racket. They were shooting their guns and yelling. They must have been doing drills. The next day they were gone. They left quite a mess in my fields but they were all gone." The men just looked at each other and nodded.

The next morning the men stood on the lake's edge and looked across to Raccoon Island through telescopes. Nothing could be seen but trees.

"It doesn't look like anyone is over there." one man in the group said.

The Lieutenant quickly looked over at him with a glare. "They are there all right."

Soon they had two row boats and were rowing over to the island. As they went across the water, the President and the General scanned the shoreline and the horizon. It is a vast lake. Eventually, they rowed up on shore.

The gravel and rocks made a thunder like sound as the bellies of the boats dragged across shore bottom. The seven men pulled their boats up and walked off the beach and into the tree line. There was an unsettling silence. The Lieutenant was nervous. The other men were standing ready with their hands on their revolvers. They didn't know what to expect. As hard as they looked, the men couldn't see the Raccoon guards that were watching them from the trees. The moment the men were close to the island the Raccoons knew they were there.

"Keep your weapons holstered," Grant said with a calming voice as he scanned the woods. "This is a peace mission." The men were silent and obedient.

All of a sudden, the Raccoons were upon them. They were surrounded by five guards dressed in armor with their short swords and repeating rifles. The group of men, including the President just stared at them in amazement. Their armor gleamed in the sunlight. They looked like true warriors. One Raccoon stepped forward and approached Lincoln. The President was, by far, the tallest man in the group. He must have looked like the leader to the Raccoon. The Raccoon had markings on his body armor that indicated he may be a ranking officer.

"What is your business here, human?"

The President swallowed hard and then gave the creature a friendly smile. He never had to face a large talking raccoon before. However, being a politician, Mr. Lincoln knew the importance of body language and was aware of his own. He made a conscious effort not to show his fear. Lincoln made direct eye contact with the Raccoon.

"I am President Abraham Lincoln. We have come here to sign a peace treaty."

"Follow me." The guard stated.

He talked to the other raccoons in raccoon chatter and they disappeared into the woods. They went ahead to tell the elders that Lincoln himself was on their island.

After walking deeper into the island's interior, the men were led to the Raccoon village. There they saw families of raccoons working and playing. They saw young males learning the skills of their ancestors and others crafting objects from hot iron. The men were amazed. A civilization of raccoons that live much like they do.

Three elders, Leonidas and Alexander met the humans. They introduced and greeted each other. Both sides were a little cautious.

"Please, come into our great lodge and sit down. Let us discuss our issues." One of the elders said.

Soon Lincoln, Grant and the three elders were sitting at a large wooden table.

"It is very brave of you to come to our island President Lincoln. We are impressed with your courage."

"Thank you. I came so that I could see for myself your magnificent culture and so that you can hear it direct from my mouth that we offer you peace not war." The President went on to say, "I have read your demands to keep your island and to live in peace. Who are we to take it from you? As long as the United States of America exists, you will have a peace treaty with it. All I ask from you is that I get my soldiers back."

Another elder nodded his head and said, "Agreed."

For the first time in just under two hundred years, humans and Raccoons sat at a table in peace. It was a historic moment.

Major General Grant laid both copies of the treaty on the table. He then read it out loud for all to hear. Both, men and raccoons smiled. President Lincoln signed both copies and the Raccoon elders put their seal of approval on both copies. When the signing was complete, Leonidas stepped forward and spoke to President Lincoln.

"Your men will be released back to their camp site." He then handed the President a map on a piece of deer skin. "Here is the location of your soldiers who died in battle."

As Lincoln took the map he looked into the eyes of Leonidas. He could tell the Raccoon had a somber feeling about what this map represented. It was good to know the Raccoons valued life as much as he did. Eventually, the men left the Island. When they left, they left as friends of the Raccoons.

The freed soldiers were put back into action and fought in the battle at Gettysburg. They were often heard saying that they would rather be at Gettysburg than at Prospect Point. No one knew what they meant by that.

Major General McClellan disappointed President Lincoln again at the Battle of Sharpsburg against the Confederates. The President relieved him of his command. His career as a commander of soldiers was short.

The soldiers who lost their lives at the Battle of Prospect Point were counted as casualties at the Battle of Antietam and given a proper military burial.

Raccoon Island was safe for now.

Chapter 9
The Dutchmen's Debt is Due

Nelson spit tobacco juice onto the floor. "Well Red Feather, that sure is one hell of a bedtime story you told us. Do you expect us to believe that there is a bunch of Raccoon warriors knocking on our door? Why I bet they are nothin more than a couple of fat old bounty hunters trying to scare us into given up ole Dutch here."

The sound of thunder cracked across the sky and rattled the glass of the one window in the shack. The storm was real close now. Red Feather sat on the floor and folded his legs under each other. He then tilted his head down so no one could see his face under the shadow of his hat. He looked like a pile of clothes on the floor.

"I don't expect you to do anything Nelson. Except die."

The man by the door chimed in. "Nelson, I seen one of them Raccoons standing out there! He tried to shoot me! I say we give Dutch up."

A couple of the other men agreed. "Ya, let's turn Dutch over." "We don't need trouble with who ever it is outside." "This isn't our fight."

Nelson looked at them with disgust. "Who are they to tell us what to do? Suppose it was one of you those fellas were looking for? Would you want us to give you up so we can save our own hides? What makes you so sure that they won't try to kill all of us anyway?"

Dutch chimed in. "Yah dis is true. Day may kill all of us!"

Dutch was desperate to get the men to be on his side. It was a selfish move. He was driven by the thought of all the money he would get for the fur he was wearing. Even at this point, Dutch didn't tell his fellow trappers what he had done and exactly who was after him. He cared about getting out alive and if he had to cause the death of a few fellow trappers then so be it.

All the men except for Red Feather thought about what Nelson had said. One man spoke up. "We are trapped in this shack. We don't know how many of them are out there. Could be two, could be ten. If we open that door we put ourselves at a disadvantage."

"Trapper." Someone from outside yelled at the shack. "Trapper, your time is up. What have you decided?"

Crack crack crack. Boom! The lightning storm was directly over them. The powerful sound shook the very air the men and Raccoons were standing in. They could hear the noise echo off the hills surrounding the lake and roll off into the distance. Cold rain started to pour down onto the tin roof of the shack.

Nelson smiled. "The weather is on our side boys. Who would want to sit out in that rain?" He then walked over to the door and shouted through it. "We aint given him up! If you want him then come in and get him!"

Nelson turned his back to the door to look at the other men. He had a big grin on his face as he scanned the room.

"Lets see what they're made of. Check your pistols and make sure those rifles are loaded and cocked back."

The men checked their weapons. They looked at the cylinders of their hand guns to see how many rounds they had. One man blew the dust off of his front sight and moved the hammer back and forth to make sure it hadn't seized on him. His gun hadn't come out of his holster in some time. Two other men were loading their war surplus muzzle loaders. They were trappers not fighters. They never felt the need to upgrade to an expensive repeating rifle. Nelson looked at Red Feather who was still sitting on the floor.

"Red Feather. Are you going to help us here or what?"

Red Feather looked up. "Dutch has taken something that was not his to take. He must answer for his actions. If you defend him then you are no better than he is."

Nelson looked down at him. "Red Feather, you will never be one of us."

Nelson pulled his pistol from his belt and turned to face the door. "Get Ready boys."

The other men fanned out across the shack and aimed their weapons toward the door. Nelson looked back at them and smiled with his stained teeth. As he did, the door suddenly came crashing off of its hinges. It hit Nelson square in the face knocking him to the floor and landing on top of him. The men in the shack opened fire and shot through the doorway out into the dark night. Smoke from the gun powder filled the shack. In seconds the men had depleted their rounds and were now reloading. With speed and precision, a line of four Raccoons entered through the doorway. The first one peeling to the left. The second one peeling to the right. Each with another Raccoon following close behind. With their weapons facing forward, they opened fire on the men standing before them. There was no time for the reloading of pistols. In a matter seconds the three men on each side of the shack fell to the floor after being shot in the chest. There were only three left. Red Feather stayed sitting on the floor as the incident unfolded around him. Dutch fell back onto a chair and dropped his pistol. Nelson lay under the door. A fifth Raccoon came through the door way and stood on the fallen door. Nelson started squirming under it. The Raccoon pointed his rifle at the door and fired it. Nelson stopped squirming. The other four Raccoons looked at their comrade with surprise. He shrugged his shoulders and moved toward Dutch.

"You are coming with us Dutchman."

With the look of fear on his face, Dutch started screaming, "no! no! no!" as two Raccoons dragged him out of the shack and into the night rain. Lightning streaked across the sky lighting up the train station. The last glimpse Red Feather ever had of Dutch was the man being escorted down toward the lake by the Raccoons.

Three Raccoons stood over Red Feather. He looked up at them. One of the warriors reached his hand out to Red Feather in order to help him stand up.

"Go in peace brother. Our grievance is not with you."

Red Feather nodded his head and stepped out into the night. The rain had stopped. The storm had passed. As Red Feather walked up the hill away from the train station, the trapper shack suddenly burst into flames. All evidence of the Raccoons being there would be destroyed.

Their secret of Raccoon Island would stay a secret, for now.

The End

Epilogue

The secret treaty between the Raccoons and the Federal Government of the United States would be passed on from president to president. Keeping man off the island would prove to be tough to do from time to time as the population around the island increased. Myth and speculation would explain away the occasional sighting of a Raccoon. Each new president came to the same conclusion. Man was not ready to know of the existence of the Raccoons.

Soon, Red Feather would come under suspicion for the murder of his fellow trappers. He would eventually be arrested and brought to trial for the crimes of multiple murders. Would a jury believe the truth of what really happened? Would Red Feather reveal the secret of the island to a judge and jury when the chance of being hung by his neck till death looms over him? Would the Raccoons do nothing while an innocent man stands trial for their actions? We shall see.

Index of real people and places

About the Author

Tim McBride is a Patrol Sergeant in the Jefferson Twp. Police Department in Jefferson Twp., NJ. He currently resides in Sparta, NJ but grew up in the Prospect Point area of Jefferson Twp. where most of his childhood activities centered around Lake Hopatcong. Growing up, the lake was a big part of his life with boating, fishing, swimming and camping all along Lake Hopatcong. As a child, the lake fueled his imagination and thirst for adventure with his friends as they explored it on homemade rafts and an aluminum rowboat he and his brother shared. Lake Hopatcong is still a source of relaxation and adventure for Tim and his family. Tim lives with his wife, son and daughter in Sparta, NJ along with their two cats and dog. This is his first novel.